W9-DCU-899

JUN 1 1 2014

Simple Experiments with

Wedges

Chris Oxlade

WINDMILL BOOKS
New York

Published in 2014 by Windmill Books, An Imprint of Rosen Publishing
29 East 21st Street, New York, NY 10010

Produced for Windmill by Calcium Creative Ltd
Editors for Calcium Creative Ltd: Sarah Eason and Jennifer Sanderson
Designer: Emma DeBanks

Photo Credits: Cover: Shutterstock: B Jones Photography. Inside: Dreamstime:
Gary Blakeley 25, Jgroup 12, Kschua 1, 23, Lighthunter 15, Lorna 24, View7 22,
Bertold Werkmann 1, Zzizar 21; Shutterstock: Ingvar Bjork 4, Carlos Caetano
9, Canismaior 20, Richard Griffin 17, JPS 7, Jupeart 16, Dominique Landau
8, Noerenberg 6, Nostal6ie 28, Ivaschenko Roman 13, Sklep Spozywczy 5,
Valentyn Volkov 29; Tudor Photography: 10, 11, 18, 19, 26, 27.

Library of Congress Cataloging-in-Publication Data

Oxlade, Chris.
Simple experiments with wedges / by Chris Oxlade.
pages cm. — (Science experiments with simple machines)
Includes index.
ISBN 978-1-61533-755-2 (library binding) — ISBN 978-1-61533-827-6 (pbk.) —
ISBN 978-1-61533-828-3 (6-pack)
1. Wedges—Experiments—Juvenile literature. 2. Force and energy—Juvenile
literature. I. Title.
TJ1201.W44O94 2014
621.8—dc23
2013003807

Manufactured in the United States of America

CPSIA Compliance Information: Batch #BS13WM: For Further Information contact Windmill Books, New York, New York at 1-866-478-0556

Contents

Simple Machines

What do you think of when you hear the word "machine?" Perhaps you imagine an aircraft, a digger, or even a computer. Machines are things that make our lives easier by helping us do jobs. Aircraft, diggers, and computers are complicated machines, made up of thousands of parts. However, many machines are very simple. They have only one or two parts. The **wedge** is one type of simple machine.

Types of Simple Machines

There are six types of simple machines. Wedges are one. The others are **levers**, **pulleys**, **wheel and axles**, **screws**, and **inclined planes**. Some of these machines do not really look like machines. Some do not have any moving parts. However, they still help us do jobs in our everyday lives.

A pair of scissors uses levers and wedges to help you cut paper.

The blade of a spade has a wedge at the front for slicing into sand or soil.

What Is a Wedge?

A wedge is a triangular-shaped piece of material. A wedge has no moving parts. Whenever you cut something with a knife, stick a pin into a notice board, or zip a zipper, wedges are helping you. In this book, you will find plenty of examples of wedges at work. There are also some interesting experiments for you to do. Try them out and discover for yourself how wedges work.

How Wedges Work

A wedge is a very simple machine. It is a piece of material in the shape of a long, thin triangle. Wedges are normally made of a hard material, such as wood, metal, or plastic, because they must be tough enough to do their jobs.

The Shape of a Wedge

A wedge works because of its triangular shape. The two sides of a wedge face away from each other. When you push a wedge into a small gap, the faces of the wedge press on the sides of the gap, pushing them apart.

This wedge-shaped ax head is splitting the wood apart.

Pushes and Pulls

In this book you will see the words **"force,"** "effort," and **"load."** A force is a push or a pull. Simple machines change the direction or **magnitude** of forces. An effort is a force that you make on a simple machine. The load is the **weight** or other force that a machine moves.

Using Wedges

When you use a wedge, the effort is the push you make on the end of the wedge. The load is the resistance of the objects you are moving, or the material into which you put the wedge. Imagine a wedge being pushed under a heavy box. The load is the weight of the box. The wedge pushes against the floor and the underside of the box, which pushes the box upward.

Builders use wedges to lift and jam things into place.

wedges at work

Now that you know how a wedge works, let's look at some examples of wedges in action. In all these examples, the wedge splits a material apart. The wedge makes it easier to split the material than it would be to split it by hand.

What Is a Chisel?

A **chisel** is a tool designed for cutting and shaping materials. It has a sharp blade with a wedge-shaped tip. When the chisel is pushed into a material, the wedge splits the material apart.

A road drill has a wedge-shaped drilling bit that breaks up concrete.

A zipper slider pushes apart the two halves of the zipper.

Using Chisels

Carpenters cut into wood using wood chisels. These chisels have very sharp blades and can be pushed into wood by hand to shave off pieces of wood. Builders and sculptors break and shape stone, brick, and concrete with really tough chisels. These chisels are hammered into the material. The wedge pushes sideways on the material with great force and splits off pieces.

Zip It!

A zipper relies on a wedge. Take a close look at a zipper to see if you can find the wedge, it is inside the zipper slider. As you unzip, the wedge pulls the two sides of the zipper apart.

9

Moving with wedges

This experiment will show you the power of wedges. When you push a simple wedge between two objects, it will push the objects apart.

1 Fill two large cardboard boxes with books to make them heavy, but not so heavy that you cannot lift them. Put the boxes next to each other on the floor, so that they are touching. Try moving them apart with your hands.

2 Try pushing the sharp end of the narrow edge of a binder (the wedge) between the two boxes. What happens to the boxes? How hard did you have to push to make the boxes move?

So Simple!

You should have found that you needed a much smaller push to move the boxes apart using the wedge than by moving them apart with your hands. The wedge increased the strength of your push.

Cutting with wedges

Knives slice through different materials, from cheese and carrots to wood and plastic. A knife has one or two sharp edges that do the cutting. These edges are actually thin wedges. When you press the blade into a material, the wedge pushes through the material, splitting it apart.

Sharp Works Best

A sharp knife cuts better than a blunt knife. When a knife is sharp, the wedge along its edge is very narrow, so it can easily push through materials. When a knife is blunt, the end of the wedge is wider, so it cannot cut so easily.

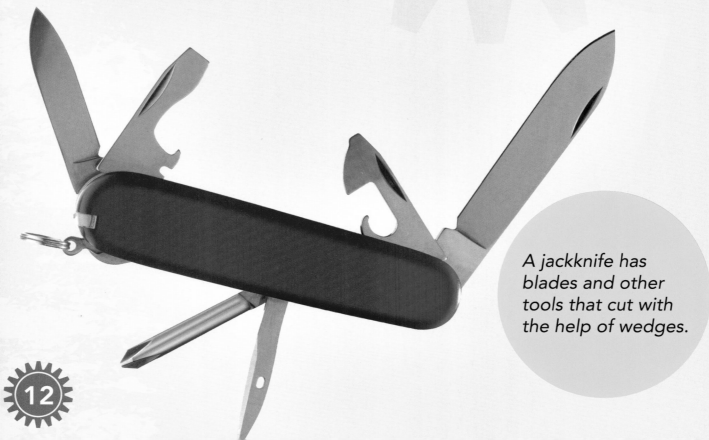

A jackknife has blades and other tools that cut with the help of wedges.

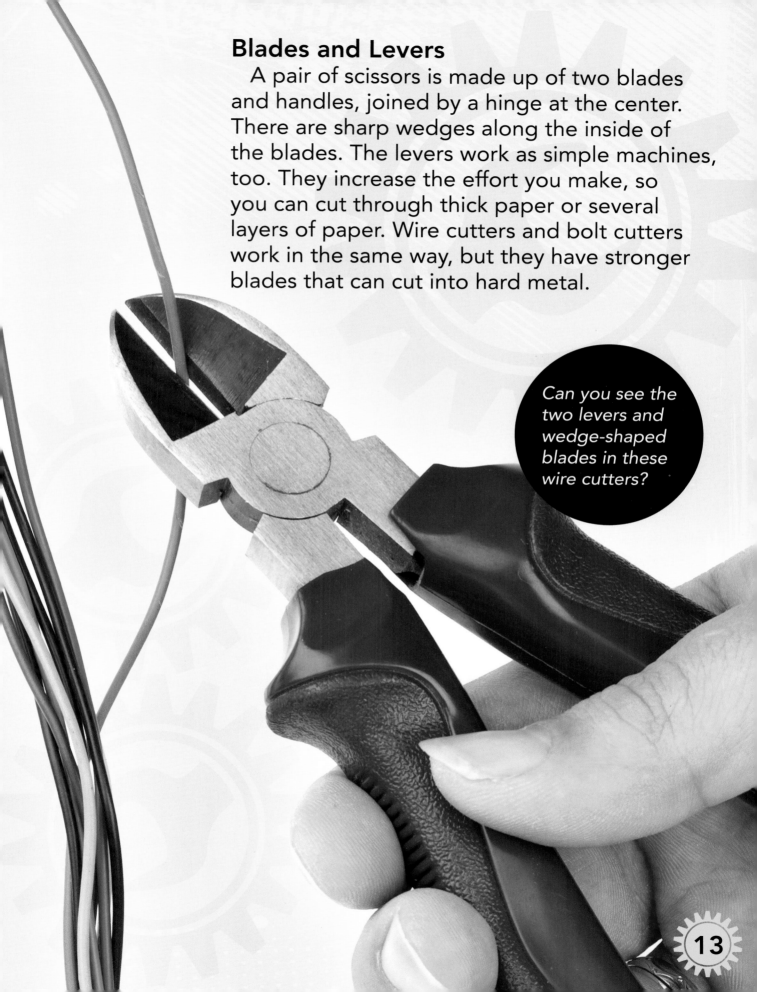

Blades and Levers

A pair of scissors is made up of two blades and handles, joined by a hinge at the center. There are sharp wedges along the inside of the blades. The levers work as simple machines, too. They increase the effort you make, so you can cut through thick paper or several layers of paper. Wire cutters and bolt cutters work in the same way, but they have stronger blades that can cut into hard metal.

Can you see the two levers and wedge-shaped blades in these wire cutters?

More Wedge Cutters

There are plenty more examples of wedges that cut materials. Take a look around your kitchen. You might find a pizza-cutting wheel, which has a sharp wedge around its **rim**. Pastry cutters also have a wedge on the underside. A can opener has a sharp wheel that slices into the can.

Cutting Wood

We use a hand ax for chopping through thin branches, or chopping up small pieces of wood. The shape of the wedge on the head of an ax is easy to see. It pushes the wood apart as the ax hits the wood. To cut thicker branches or small trees, or to chop up big logs, we use an ax with a heavier head and longer handle.

The wedge-shaped head of an ax easily splits logs in half.

Your mouth is full of wedges, your teeth! They split off pieces of food.

Sawing Through Objects

A saw is a tool for cutting through hard wood, plastic, or metal. A saw blade has many small teeth along its edge. Each one of these teeth is a tiny wedge with sharp edges. When you pull the saw backward and forward, the wedges push downward into the material, splitting it apart.

Teeth as Wedges

Your front teeth, called incisors, are shaped like wedges. They work like chisels. Their job is to bite off pieces of food. For example, when you bite into an apple, your incisors push the apple's flesh apart, breaking off a piece. The effort to push your teeth into the apple comes from muscles in your jaw.

Sharp Points

Think about the sharp point at the end of a skewer, knitting needle, or nail. Can you see that the point is like a wedge? A sharp point works in the same way as a wedge, pushing sideways when it is forced into a material.

Pins and Needles

Pins and needles are used in sewing. Pins hold pieces of fabric together, and needles pull threads through fabric. Both are very thin, and have very sharp points that work as tiny wedges. When you push a needle or pin into a fabric, the wedge pushes the fabric apart to let the needle or pin through.

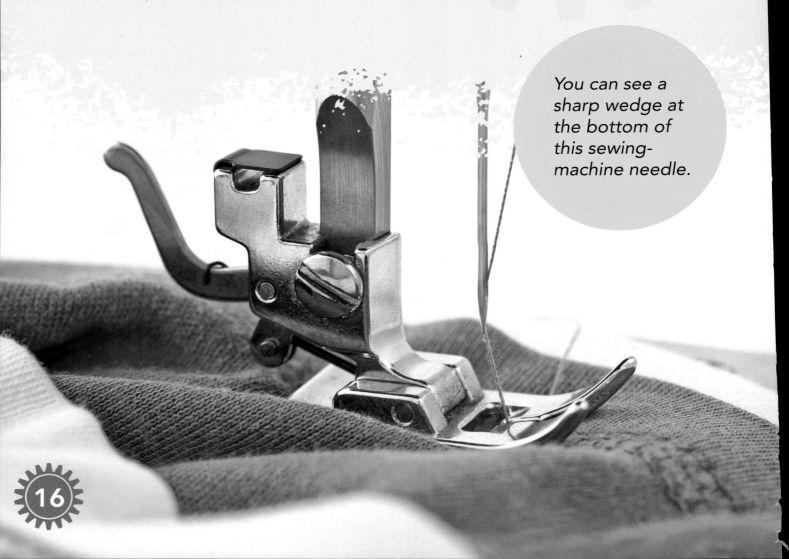

You can see a sharp wedge at the bottom of this sewing-machine needle.

Making Holes

Sometimes we need to make holes in pieces of material. Tools for making holes include the **bradawl** for making small holes in wood, the **awl** for making holes in leather, and the dibber (also called a dibble), for making holes in soil to plant seeds and seedlings.

The pointed end of a dibber pushes the soil apart to make a hole for a seed.

Nails for Fixing

Nails fix pieces of wood together, or fix things to wood. The point of a nail is a wedge. When you hit a nail with a hammer, you make a very big push on the end of the nail. The nail's wedge makes an even bigger sideways push on the tough wood, splitting it apart so that the nail can move forward.

Blunt and Sharp

The blades of knives and the points of pins are wedges. Try this experiment to compare sharp blades and points with blunt ones.

1 Place a small block of cheese on a cutting board. Hold a kitchen knife with the sharp edge of the blade pointing upward. Try to cut the cheese. Try to cut the cheese again, this time with the sharp edge of the knife pointing downward.

You Will Need:

- Cheese
- A cutting board
- A kitchen knife (ask an adult before you use this)
- A paper clip
- A pin

18

2 Unbend a paper clip. Try pushing the end of the clip down into the cheese. Now, try pushing a sharp pin into the cheese instead. Which was easier to push into the cheese?

So Simple!

Cutting the cheese with the sharp edge of a knife was easier than cutting it with the blunt edge. This is because the sharp edge is a wedge that pushed the cheese apart. The pin was easier to push into the cheese than the paper clip because its end is a wedge.

wedges in the past

People have known about wedges for millions of years. The wedge was probably the first simple machine that people invented, although for most of that time, people did not realize the wedge was a simple machine.

Chopping and Cutting

Wedges were important tools during a time called the Stone Age. At the time, people lived by hunting animals and searching for fruits and berries. They made simple cutting tools by chipping away pieces of rock to form sharp edges. With these tools they skinned and cut up the animals that they caught.

This ancient stone ax head has a wedge at one end.

Wedge

The wedge on this traditional plow was used to cut through the soil.

Plowing the Land

The plow is another important tool that has been in use for many thousands of years. Wedges on a plow dig into the soil as the plow moves along, loosening the soil and making furrows ready for planting crops. The earliest plows were simply sticks pushed through soil by hand, but later, plows were pulled by animals.

Ship Wedges

Wedges had many other uses in history. The ancient Romans and Greeks built fighting ships called galleys. These ships had huge wooden wedges on the **bow**, which smashed holes in the hulls of enemy ships.

Jamming with Wedges

When you push a wedge between two objects, the wedge turns a small effort into a larger, sideways push. The wedge normally pushes the objects apart. What happens if you push a wedge in and the objects cannot move? The answer is that the wedge pushes hard against the objects, and then will not move farther. It gets stuck, and it stops the objects from moving together again.

Friction at Work

Wedges jam in place because of a force called **friction**. Friction tries to stop surfaces that are touching from sliding past each other. The greater the force that pushes the surfaces together, the greater the friction between them. When you jam a wedge into a gap, the sides of the wedge push hard against the sides of the gap. Friction stops the wedge coming out again.

These wooden wedges are jammed in to stop the upper concrete slab from dropping down.

Door Wedges

A door wedge is an everyday example of a wedge jamming things. A door wedge is a wooden or rubber wedge that slides into the small gap under a door. The wedge presses hard against the bottom of the door and against the floor underneath. Then, friction between the wedge, the door, and the floor, stops the door from opening or closing.

A door wedge must have a narrow end to slide into the gap under a door.

moving with wedges

Wedges are also useful for moving materials around. They can make large forces on loose, solid materials, such as snow or soil, and also on water. When you push a wedge into a loose material or into water, the wedge pushes it sideways. Here are some examples of how wedges move things.

Snow Plows

A snow plow pushes snow to the side just as a farm plow pushes soil to the side. A snow-plow truck has a blade on the front that is a wedge. As the truck moves forward, the blade pushes into the snow. The blade turns the forward push into a sideways push on the snow, which throws the snow to the side of the road.

A wedge-shaped snow plow pushes snow to the sides of a highway to make it safe for motorists.

Water is thrown to the sides as the wedge-shaped bow of this boat moves forward.

Wedges in Transport

As a ship moves through the ocean, it pushes water out of the way. At the front of most ships there is a wedge-shaped bow. As the engine pushes a ship forward, the sides of the bow push the water to the sides, to let the ship slide through it. Fast cars and express trains use the same trick. They have wedge-shaped front ends, which push the air aside as they speed along.

Jamming a Door

In this experiment you see how wedges work to stop a door from opening or closing by accident.

1 Find a door that has at least a ½-inch-(12-mm) gap under it when it is open. Open the door about halfway.

2 Prop up one edge of the thin book with some books to make a steep ramp, and position the ramp with its edge under the door. Now, try shutting the door. What happens?

3 Take away some of the books to make the ramp more shallow (less steep). Now try to shut the door again. What happens this time?

So Simple!

The ramp acted as a wedge under the door. With the steeply sloping ramp, the books probably slid across the floor. With the shallow ramp, the books should have jammed against the floor. A longer, narrower wedge was better for jamming, because it pressed harder on the door and floor.

Amazing Machines

Wedges are simple, but handy, machines. They make our lives easier by increasing the effort we make. The sharp points of wedges allow us to easily cut, shape, and pierce materials. Other wedges allow us to move materials around easily, and to jam things in place.

What Did You Learn?

Have you tried the simple experiments in the book? What did you learn about wedges?

In Big Machines

Wedges are simple machines that work on their own. We also find them in more complicated machines. Many machines have parts that are wedges, which do the same job as the wedges we have seen. Examples of these include mechanical diggers, which have wedge-shaped teeth on their buckets, and street drills, which use a wedge to break up concrete.

The bucket of a mechanical digger has wedges that slice into soil.

This fork has four wedge-shaped prongs that push into a sausage!

Can't Live Without Them

Humans have been using wedges for millions of years. Wedges might be simple, but it would be almost impossible for us to live without them. We have seen many wedges in this book, but there are plenty more! For example, there are many garden tools that have wedges for piercing soil, and forks have wedges for picking up food. Keep an eye out for wedges at work wherever you go!

Glossary

awl (OL) A sharp, pointed tool used to punch holes in leather or wood.

bow (BOW) The front end of a ship or boat.

bradawl (BRAD-ol) A tool with a tough metal spike, used to make small holes in wood before putting in a screw.

chisel (CHIH-zul) A metal tool with a sharp wedge at the tip, used to cut and shape wood or stone.

force (FORS) A push or a pull.

friction (FRIK-shin) The force that tries to stop two surfaces from sliding over each other.

inclined planes (in-KLYND-PLAYNS) Slopes used as simple machines.

levers (LEH-vurs) Rods or bars used as a simple machines.

load (LOHD) The push or pull that a lever overcomes, which may be the weight of an object.

magnitude (MAG-nih-tood) The measurement of something's strength.

pulleys (PU-leez) Wheels with ropes around them that work as simple machines.

rim (RIM) The outside edge of a disk.

screws (SKROOZ) Simple machines with inclined planes wrapped around cyclinders.

wedge (WEJ) A triangular object used as a simple machine.

weight (WAYT) The force of gravity on an object, which pulls the object downward.

wheel and axles (WEEL AND AK-sulz) Simple machines made up of disks with fixed bars running through their centers.

Read More

To learn more about wedges, check out these interesting books:

Christiansen, Jennifer. *Get to Know Wedges*. Get to Know Simple Machines. New York: Crabtree Publishing Company, 2009.

Gosman, Gillian. *Wedges in Action*. Simple Machines at Work. New York: PowerKids Press, 2010.

Roza, Greg. *Wedges*. Simple Machine Science. New York: Gareth Stevens Publishing, 2013.

Tomljanovic, Tatiana. *Wedges*. Science Matters: Simple Machines. New York: Weigl Publishers, 2009.

Yasuda, Anita. *Explore Simple Machines!* Explore Your World. White River Junction, Vermont: Nomad Press, 2011.

Websites

For web resources related to the subject of this book, go to: www.windmillbooks.com/weblinks and select this book's title.

31

Index